Karen's Book

Little Sister

Karen's Book
Ann M. Martin

Illustrations by Susan Crocca Tang

A
LITTLE APPLE
PAPERBACK

SCHOLASTIC INC.
New York Toronto London Auckland Sydney

ISBN 0-590-50051-1

12 11 10 9 8 7 6 5 4 3 2 1   8 9/9 0 1 2 3/0

Printed in the U.S.A.   40
First Scholastic printing, August 1998

The author gratefully acknowledges
Stephanie Calmenson
for her help
with this book.

Is Anybody Home?

I was sitting at the kitchen table blowing bubbles in my milk. *Blubble. Blubble. Blubble.*

"Bubboos!" said my little sister, Emily Michelle.

I blew a little harder to impress her. The bubbles spilled over my glass, onto the table, and down to the floor.

"You made a mess," said David Michael, my stepbrother.

"I will help you clean up," said Nannie, my stepgrandmother. "Then I have to get back to work."

Nannie has her own candy-making business. She works out of our second kitchen. (It used to be our pantry.)

While Nannie and I were cleaning up, Emily decided to blow bubbles too. But she did not do it right. That is because she is only two and a half. Instead of blowing, she snorted up some of her milk. The next thing we knew, she was coughing up the milk and her cup was on the floor.

After cleaning up the new mess, Nannie took Emily back to the kitchen with her. That left David Michael and me. We had been playing together all morning. We were kind of tired of each other.

"I am going upstairs to read a book," said David Michael. That left just me.

Daddy was in his office working. He works at home, like Nannie. When the door to his office is closed it means I am not supposed to bother him if I can help it. (The door was closed.)

Elizabeth, my stepmother, was at her office downtown.

Mommy and Seth, who is my stepfather, and Andrew, who is my little brother (he is four going on five), were in Chicago. (I will tell you why very soon.)

Kristy, my stepsister, was at her friend Abby's beach house.

Charlie and Sam, my other stepbrothers, were at sleepaway camp. (They were counselors.)

My best friend Hannie Papadakis had gone to visit her aunt in the country. And my other best friend, Nancy Dawes, was with her family at the shore.

So I was alone on a Friday afternoon in August. I was B-O-R-E-D. That spells bored! I could not believe it. I am usually a very busy person.

Who am I? My name is Karen Brewer. I am seven years old. I have blonde hair, blue eyes, and a bunch of freckles. (I have more freckles in the summertime because of the sun.) I am a glasses-wearer. I have two pairs. I have a blue pair for reading. I have a pink pair to wear the rest of the time. I do not have prescription sunglasses yet. But maybe I will. That will make three pairs of glasses!

Anyway, that is who I am. The question now was, what am I going to do? Hmm . . . I know! I promised to tell you why Mommy, Seth, and Andrew are in Chicago. Are you ready? It is a long story.

A Tale of Two Cities

The story I have to tell you starts when I was very little. You already know some of it, but now I will tell you more.

Back when I was little, my family was little too. It was just Mommy, Daddy, Andrew, and me. We all lived together in a big house in Stoneybrook, Connecticut.

Then Mommy and Daddy started having troubles. They argued all the time. They tried to work things out but they just could not do it. So they explained to Andrew and me that they love each of us very much, but they could not live together anymore. And they got divorced. Mommy moved to a little house not far away in Stoneybrook. She took Andrew and me with her. Then she met Seth. She and Seth got married, which is how Seth became my stepfather. My family had grown a little bigger.

After the divorce, Daddy stayed in the big house. (It is the house he grew up in.) He met Elizabeth and they got married. Elizabeth had been married once before and had four children. They are my stepsister and stepbrothers, Kristy, David Michael, Sam, and Charlie. Kristy is thirteen and the best stepsister ever. David Michael is seven, like me. And Sam and Charlie are so old they are in high school.

After awhile Daddy and Elizabeth adopted Emily from a faraway country called Vietnam. That is when Nannie came to live with us.

Nannie is Elizabeth's mother. She came to help out with Emily, but she really helps the whole family.

So that is how I started out with a little family and wound up with a big family. And I have not even told you about the pets yet. There are lots of them!

Midgie is Seth's dog, and Rocky is Seth's cat. Emily Junior is my pet rat. (I named her after Emily, of course.) Bob is Andrew's hermit crab.

The pets at the big house are Shannon, David Michael's Bernese mountain dog puppy; Scout, our training-to-be-a-guide-dog puppy; Boo-Boo, Daddy's cranky old cat; Crystal Light the Second, my goldfish; and Goldfishie, Andrew's llama . . . I mean fish.

Andrew and I used to switch houses almost every month. We spent one month at the big house and one month at the little house.

I gave us special names because we each have two of so many things. I started calling us Andrew Two-Two and Karen Two-Two. (I thought up those names after my teacher,

Ms. Colman, read a book to our class. It was called *Jacob Two-Two Meets the Hooded Fang*.)

We each have two families with two mommies and two daddies. We have two sets of toys and clothes and books. And we both have two bicycles, one at each house. I also have two best friends, Hannie and Nancy. Hannie lives across the street and one house over from the big house. Nancy lives next door to the little house.

Then came Chicago, which is why I started to tell you this story in the first place. What happened is that Seth, who is a carpenter, was offered an excellent job in Chicago that would last for a few months. He tried commuting for a while. That means he flew back and forth between work in Chicago and home in Stoneybrook. That was hard on all of us. So Mommy, Seth, Andrew, me — plus Midgie, Rocky, Emily Junior, and Bob — moved to Chicago. Now I had two cities on top of everything else — Stoneybrook and Chicago.

But I missed being in Stoneybrook very much. So I moved back. And here I am alone in the kitchen at the big house and I am B-O-R-E-D, which spells bored. What am I going to do now?

Karen's Idea

I decided David Michael had a good idea when he went upstairs to read. I went to my room to do the same thing. And I knew just the book I wanted to read.

Kristy had been reading some of the Little House books to me. (I told you she is the best stepsister ever.) The Little House books were written by Laura Ingalls Wilder, and they tell about her life. She was a real and true American pioneer. I love her books.

I picked up the first one, *Little House in the Big Woods*, and looked at the pictures. When she was a little girl, Laura lived with her ma, pa, and two sisters in a small log cabin. Her pa built the cabin himself. It was a lot smaller than my little house, but five people lived in it.

The three girls slept in trundle beds. (Those are little beds that slide underneath a big bed.) They helped their ma make cheese and butter. Their pa hunted, farmed, played his fiddle, and sang to his family. Laura Ingalls Wilder had a happy and exciting life.

I thought of someone else I know who has a happy and exciting life — well, most of the time. Me!

I do not sleep in a trundle bed or churn butter (except once, for a school cooking project). But I do other exciting things.

Hmm. Maybe I could write the story of *my* life the way Laura Ingalls Wilder wrote the story of hers. Only I would illustrate my story too. The book would be about me, Karen Brewer, and my family and friends because they are part of my life too. Ooh! This was a gigundoly good idea.

12

Where would I start? I decided to start with the day I was born. That was a long time ago. Seven years. I did not remember much. In fact, I did not remember anything about the day I was born. Mommy and Daddy had told me stories, though. And I knew Daddy had pictures. I needed to do some research.

I ran downstairs to Daddy's office. His door was still closed.

I stood there deciding what to do. Knock. Do not knock. Knock. Do not knock.

Finally I felt as though I would burst if I did not knock on the door. Bursting would be an emergency situation. I knew Daddy would not want me to burst. Okay. I had to knock. I could not help it.

Knock, knock!

"Come in," replied Daddy.

I opened the door a crack and peeked in.

"I am sorry to bother you when you are working," I said. "But I really could not help it."

"That is all right," said Daddy. "I was just

13

about finished anyway. What can I do for you?"

"You can help me with some research," I replied.

"Sure," said Daddy. "What kind of research?"

"I am going to write my life story. I need to look at my baby book."

"You have come to the right place," said Daddy. "I keep it here in my office."

Yes! I was going to start my research right away. And I did not even have to burst.

Karen's History Lesson

My baby book was white with pink lettering. The very first page was titled BABY'S FAMILY TREE. I had not seen it in a long time.

"There are a few branches missing from this tree," I said.

"You are right," Daddy replied. "Your tree has grown since Mommy and I wrote in this book."

It was still fun to look at. I found names of people I know and love, and names of people I have never met. But they were all part of my history. I turned the page. There was a picture of me as a smiling baby.

"Hey, I was cute!" I said.

"You still are," replied Daddy.

"You know what is funny? I had no hair in the picture, but I have a lot now. You and Mommy had lots of hair in the picture, but you do not have so much now," I said.

"Karen Brewer, did you take my hair?" asked Daddy, joking. "I want it back!"

I leafed through a few more pages. I saw myself growing bigger and bigger.

"May I borrow the book?" I asked.

"Of course you may," replied Daddy. "I also have some other things that might interest you."

He pulled out a box and opened it. It was full of drawings I made when I was little. Some of them were just scribbles.

"You were a very good artist for your age, Karen," said Daddy. "You were a good writer too. You could not write down the words yourself, but you told your stories to

Mommy and me. We wrote them down for you."

Daddy showed me one of my stories. It was about shopping at the supermarket with Mommy.

Karen go to market with Mommy. Buy milk. Buy eggs. Buy cookies. Eat cookies! Love cookies! The end.

"Thank goodness I am a better writer now," I said. "Okay. I need to know all about the day I was born. I know you and Mommy have told me the story lots of times. But I may have forgotten some things."

"Ask me any questions," said Daddy. "I will answer the best I can."

"Okay," I replied. "Here goes."

I had a long list of questions. I wanted to know exactly what the weather was like on the day I was born. What time was I born? How much did I weigh? How tall was I? Who were my first visitors? Did I cry much?

I asked Daddy all my questions and he answered them for me one by one. We even called Mommy in Chicago to see if there was anything else she wanted to tell me. By the time we were done, I knew the whole story of the day I was born. And I had lots of other stories too.

Decisions, Decisions

I carried my baby book upstairs. I was ready to begin writing. Watch out, Laura Ingalls Wilder!

I grabbed a pencil and a sheet of paper from my desk. I looked at the pencil and paper. They were not in great shape. The pencil was short and chewed. (I wondered whose pencil it was. I do not chew my pencils.) Hardly any eraser was left. And the sheet of paper I picked was creased in one corner.

I decided I was not ready to begin writing

after all. A person's life story is a very important document and it should be beautifully written.

I found a brand-new pencil. It was pink with white flowers. Nannie had given it to me the week before. (Nannie was not even on my family tree. I would have to fix that.) Then I found clean paper with no creases.

I took my paper and pencil to my bed. It is a cozy place to write.

"Move over, please, Moosie and Goosie," I said.

Moosie and Goosie are my stuffed cats who look exactly the same. Goosie usually lives at the little house, but was with me at the big house while the rest of my family was in Chicago. I was glad Moosie and Goosie were getting along so well.

I puffed up my pillows and leaned back. I was finally ready. In the middle of the first page, I wrote in big letters:

MY LIFE STORY
BY KAREN BREWER

I took another sheet of paper and wrote at the top:

THE DAY I WAS BORN

Then I began my story.

IT WAS A DARK AND STORMY NIGHT WHEN...

No. That was not right. Daddy said I was born on a warm spring day. But that did not sound so exciting. Maybe the real and true story needed a little help. I tried again.

IT WAS THE MOST BEAUTIFUL SPRING DAY IN HISTORY. THE WEATHER ANNOUNCER WAS TALKING ABOUT HOW AMAZING THE WEATHER WAS ON THIS DAY.

Hmm. Maybe that was too much. Daddy had not said anything about the weather announcer. I tried again:

IT WAS A BEAUTIFUL SPRING DAY. PEOPLE EVERYWHERE WERE TALKING ABOUT IT. "WHAT A BEAUTIFUL DAY TO BE BORN!" SAID A MAN ON THE STREET. "YES, I WISH I COULD HAVE BEEN BORN ON A DAY LIKE TODAY," SAID A WOMAN.

I looked at Moosie and Goosie. I could tell

they did not believe my story. I erased the last three sentences. Here is what was left:

IT WAS A BEAUTIFUL SPRING DAY.

That was the real and true story. You know what? It was not a bad way to start. I decided to tell my story the way it really happened. All I had to do was figure out what to say next.

I looked at one of my baby pictures. I closed my eyes and made believe I was a baby again. I imagined everyone going wild. They were holding me, feeding me, and — *ooh!* — they were tickling me!

Wait a minute. I was going too fast. Before I was tickled, I had to be born. Mommy and Daddy had told me about that day lots of times. And now Daddy had answered my questions. I was finally ready to begin my story.

The Day I Was Born:
Part One

It was a beautiful spring day. Mommy and Daddy were up bright and early even though it was the weekend.

"Good morning, Lisa," said Daddy. "How are you feeling?"

"I am fine, thank you," replied Mommy.

Daddy looked down at Mommy's belly.

"And how are you feeling this morning, Baby?" he asked.

Mommy smiled. "Baby seems to be just fine," she said.

"Would the two of you like me to make breakfast for you?" asked Daddy.

"We would love it!" replied Mommy.

Daddy made pancakes with sliced strawberries on top. He drank a cup of coffee. Mommy drank a glass of milk.

"Would you like to go for a walk?" asked Mommy. "It is beautiful out, and I am feeling restless."

"That sounds good to me," replied Daddy. "We can stop at some Saturday-morning yard sales. Who knows what we will find?"

Mommy put on a sweater. She could not button it because her belly was too big. Mommy and Daddy went outside, holding hands. It was still very early, but they were not the only ones out.

"Good morning!" called a gray-haired man, walking a gray-haired dog. "When do you think your baby will be born?"

"Any day now," replied Daddy proudly.

At the corner, a woman on her bicycle

stopped to wait for the light. She looked at Mommy and Daddy and smiled.

"What are you going to name your baby?" she asked.

"We are going to wait and meet our baby before we pick a name," said Mommy.

"Do you think it is a boy or a girl?" asked the woman.

"We will be happy either way!" said Daddy.

The light changed. "Good luck," called the woman as she rode ahead.

"Look, there is a sign for a yard sale up ahead," said Mommy.

The sale was in the backyard of a small house. Right away Mommy and Daddy saw something they both loved. It was a beautiful old rocking chair, sitting on the grass in the sun.

"We can rock our baby in that chair," said Mommy. "It is perfect!"

"I love that chair too," replied Daddy. "But I do not want to buy it now. Some people say it is unlucky to buy too many things for a baby before it is born."

"But the chair may not be here if we wait," said Mommy. "Anyway, it does not have to be for our baby. We have a big house and can always use an extra chair."

"Well, maybe you are right," said Daddy.

"No. We will wait," said Mommy. "We can always find another pretty chair."

Mommy and Daddy kept changing their minds. They were rocking back and forth like the you-know-what. Just then, the owner of the house saw them.

"Hi, folks," he said. "How are you today? I will be happy to answer your questions. I know this chair well."

"Oh, my," said Mommy. "I need to sit down. I hope you do not mind." She sat in the rocking chair.

Daddy knelt down beside her. "Are you all right?"

"I am fine. I think our baby is ready to be born. That is all," replied Mommy, smiling.

"Oh, my," said Daddy.

"Oh, my," said the man. "We will get you to the hospital right away."

Daddy helped Mommy into the man's car. Soon they were on their way. And so was I.

The Day I Was Born:
Part Two

I did not arrive for a few more hours. The doctor checked in on Mommy every fifteen minutes.

"You are doing fine," Dr. Bradley told Mommy. "It will not be long now."

Daddy and Mommy talked a lot while they waited — mostly about me, of course. Then, in the middle of a sentence, Mommy stopped and said, "Watson, it is time!"

Mommy and Daddy were very excited.

At 2:35 in the afternoon, I, Karen Brewer, was finally born. It was my first important job. And I love important jobs.

But I need to back up a little. My name was not Karen yet. Mommy and Daddy were still calling me Baby. They looked at their list of possible names. I could also have been Arlene, Joanna, Bethany, Katherine, or Erica. I like all those names. I would have had a very hard time deciding on one.

Mommy and Daddy looked at the list again. Then they looked at me.

"There is only one name that seems right to me," said Daddy. "That name is Karen. It means 'pure.' And seeing our baby, I feel pure joy."

"Me too," said Mommy. "It is the right name."

Then they kissed my cheeks and said, "Hello, Karen Brewer. Welcome to the world!"

Mommy stayed overnight at the hospital. Daddy went home and called lots of relatives and friends. They all came to the hospital the next morning for my day-after-

being-born party. Grandma and Grandpa Packett, Mommy's parents, were there.

"We cannot get enough of our new grand-daughter!" they said.

Grandma Brewer was there too. (Daddy's father, my Grandpa Brewer, died before I was born.)

"You are the sweetest thing," said Grandma Brewer.

By the time everyone left, the room was filled with balloons and flowers and baskets of fruit. I was the star of the party. I love being the star! But I cannot remember one thing about it. I am sure I had a good time, though. Daddy took lots of pictures and I think I am smiling. (It is hard to tell because I am mostly covered up with a blanket.) Anyway, the pictures are in my baby book now.

In the afternoon Mommy and Daddy took me home. One of Daddy's friends had decorated the car with pink streamers. (There is a picture of the car in my baby book too.)

We were all buckled up. I sat in my own baby seat. Daddy drove extra carefully.

"I can hardly wait to get Karen settled in her new room," said Daddy as he turned the corner to our street.

"Look!" said Mommy. "Karen's new room is going to have something very special in it."

There it was. Sitting on the grass in the sun. The beautiful oak rocking chair.

Daddy helped Mommy and me out of the car.

"There is a note on the chair," said Mommy. She read it out loud:

This chair was in my family for a long time. My mother and father rocked me in it. I want the chair to have a special home. It belongs with you.
Your friend and neighbor,
John Washington

You know what? We still have that rocking chair. It is in the den and it is my very favorite chair.

Karen Says, "No!"

I forgot to tell one thing about the rocking chair. The way it looks now is not exactly the way it looked when we bought it. (Daddy says he will fix it up one of these days to look like new.) Here are some of the things that happened to it:

Shannon, David Michael's puppy, thought the bottom rung would be a good chewing stick, and she chewed it right off.

Once, when I was about two years old, I decided the chair would look pretty with pictures on the seat, so I found a pen and scribbled. (It was all I could do back then.) I pressed really hard and the scribbles are still there.

Then there was the time I rammed my toy car into the chair. If you look at the bottom, you can see where I hit it.

And once I sat in the chair with my doll and started rocking her.

"Ride, dolly, ride!" I said.

I rocked so hard I tipped the chair over. It banged into the window ledge. You can see those marks on the chair too.

"It sounds like I was a busy baby!" I said to Mommy and Daddy one day when I was still little.

"Yes, you were," replied Mommy. "You played with your toys, chased Boo-Boo, and put on lots of shows for Daddy and me."

"You were the center of attention most of the time," said Daddy.

I am sure I liked that a lot. I still like being the center of attention. I guess that is why I was not too happy when I found out a new baby was on the way. This is how I figured it out.

"Mommy is getting fat!" I said when I was two and a half.

Mommy said she was not getting fat. She said a baby was growing inside her. "Just the way you grew inside me."

"There is no new baby," I announced. "I am the baby."

"The new baby will be your brother or sister," replied Mommy.

"No. No brother. No sister. I am the baby."

"Your baby brother or sister will grow up to be your friend," said Mommy. "You can play together."

"No."

"You can tell each other secrets."

"No."

"We think of the new baby as a gift to you," said Daddy.

"Gift?" I said.

"That is right," said Mommy.

"You will get to be a big sister," added Daddy.

I liked that idea.

"So do you think you might like the new baby?" asked Mommy.

"No!" I replied.

Poor Mommy and Daddy. They tried very hard.

Karen Brewer, Big Sister

It did not matter whether I wanted a baby brother or sister. I was getting one anyway.

Here is what happened the day Andrew came home from the hospital. Mommy and Daddy told me some of those things. I remembered the rest all by myself.

Grandma and Grandpa Packett did not go to the hospital when Andrew was born. They were busy taking care of me. We had fun. I helped Grandma bake a welcome-home cake. I got to pour sugar and flour in a bowl. I got to mix them up with a big wooden spoon.

"Mmm. Mommy and Daddy will love the cake," I said.

After it was baked, Grandma wrote a message on top with blue icing.

"What does it say?" I asked.

I thought it would say, "Welcome Home, Mommy and Daddy." It did not. It said, "Welcome Home, Andrew!"

"No!" I cried. I reached out to wipe the letters off with my finger. Grandma picked up the cake before I could get to it.

"You must wait to eat the icing on the cake," she said. "But you may lick it out of the bowl."

By the time I finished, my face was covered with blue icing and I had forgotten about the message on the cake.

"Who wants a horsey ride?" asked Grandpa Packett.

"Me!" I said.

I climbed on Grandpa Packett's back.

"Giddyap!" I called. We galloped around

the house. I was still on his back when I heard the key in the door. Daddy hurried in and swooped me up in a big hug. Then I looked at Mommy. She was carrying my baby brother.

He was wrapped in a yellow blanket. It looked like *my* baby blanket. That was the first problem. The second problem was his face. It was a red, wrinkly prune face.

"This is Andrew, your new baby brother," said Mommy.

I squirmed out of Daddy's arms and ran away crying. That made the baby cry. Mommy carried him inside and sat down in the rocking chair.

"*My* chair!" I said. I cried harder.

Mommy handed Andrew to Daddy. Then she took me on her lap and rocked me till I stopped crying.

"It is all right. You do not have to be happy about having a brother now," said Mommy. "You are a good girl and Daddy and I love you very much. We always will."

We rocked together in the chair for a long time.

Things got better after that. People came over with presents for Andrew. Sometimes they brought presents for me too!

Then one day Andrew started crying and would not stop. Mommy had fed him. Daddy had changed him. It was not his nap time. Grandma Packett was there.

"Call the doctor," she said.

"I do not think he is sick," said Mommy.

"He was all right a minute ago," said Daddy.

While they were talking, I tiptoed to Andrew's crib. I looked down at him. He was crying so hard that his face was purple. He looked like a purple, wrinkly prune. He opened his eyes and stared at me. I made a wrinkly prune face at him.

Andrew stopped crying. I made an even funnier face. Andrew smiled. Mommy, Daddy, and Grandma Packett ran to us.

"What happened?" asked Mommy. "Andrew looks fine now."

"I think his big sister helped him," said Daddy.

"Thank you, Karen," said Mommy. She hugged me.

I looked at Andrew again. He did not look like a purple prune anymore. He looked pink and kind of cute. I, Karen Brewer, his big sister, had made him stop crying. I felt like a Gigundoly Important Person. I decided that being a big sister might not be so bad after all.

Little Friends
Day School

Being the big sister has always meant doing a lot of things first. I got born first. I got rocked in the rocking chair first. I got to use the crib first. And I got to go to school first.

On my first morning of school, I was sitting at the breakfast table with Mommy, Daddy, and Andrew, who was in his high chair.

"I am going to Little Friends Day School," I said to Andrew. "You are too young to go to school."

"Ga, ga," replied Andrew. He was too young to talk.

"I am glad you are looking forward to school, Karen," said Mommy. "I think you will have fun."

"You will color and look at books," said Daddy. "You will dance and sing and make new friends."

I could hardly wait! I ate my cereal as fast as I could. I liked Krispy Krunchies. I still do. Only when I was little I did not like them crunchy. So Mommy poured the milk onto the cereal before I sat down at the table. That way it was nice and soggy when I was ready to eat it.

"Come, Karen," said Mommy. "We do not want to be late on your first day of school."

I put on my new Ms. Frizzle backpack. There was not much in it. A snack and maybe a pencil. But I loved it. It made me feel grown-up.

Mommy was going to drive me to school. We climbed in the car and buckled up. I waved good-bye to Andrew. If he could have, I bet he would have said, "I want to go to school too!"

But I am the big sister. So I got to go.

I thought school would be great. I liked our bright, sunny room. I saw lots of games and books.

My teacher, Ms. Herman, was very nice. She talked to us. She gave me my own cubby with my name on it. I hung my Ms. Frizzle bag on the hook. Then Mommy hugged me.

"Have a good time. I will pick you up at eleven-thirty," she said.

That is when I stopped liking school. Mommy tried to leave. I grabbed her leg and would not let her go.

"Karen, what is wrong?" asked Mommy.

"I want you to stay with me," I replied.

"Mothers do not go to school," said Mommy. "I have to go home and take care of Andrew."

"Why does Andrew get to stay home? I want to stay home too," I said. "I am scared to stay here alone."

"You are not alone. Ms. Herman is here. And there are lots of other children. They can be your friends."

Just then a little girl ran across the room to me. She slipped her hand in mine.

"Hi, my name is Hannie. Do you want to play?" she asked.

I had seen Hannie before. She had just moved into my neighborhood. She seemed nice. And she was not scared.

I turned to Mommy.

"You will not forget to pick me up, will you?" I asked. (Hey, I was only a little kid. I would not be such a scaredy-cat today.)

"Of course I will pick you up," said Mommy. "I will be here at eleven-thirty."

"Come on," said Hannie. "I want to build a block castle."

"We can build towers and bridges," I said.

And that is what we did. We built towers and bridges. We sat together at story time and snack time. I had a new school and a new friend too.

Karen's Tea Party

Hannie and I became best friends. We played together all the time. We were so glad we lived across the street from each other.

That is why I was extra sad when Mommy and Daddy got divorced and I had to move away. On moving day, Hannie came to say good-bye.

"I will never see you again!" she cried.

"You will see each other every day at school," said Daddy.

"I will call you." I sniffled.

"I will drive you here to visit," said Mommy. "And I am sure Hannie's mommy and daddy will drive her to our new house. It is not so far away."

Mommy and Andrew and I climbed into our car. I thought we were going to drive to the other end of the earth. But you know what? The ride took only a few minutes.

I really did miss having my best friend close by, though. One day I wanted to have a tea party. If Hannie and I still lived across the street from each other, Mommy could have walked me to her house. But Mommy was busy and could not stop to drive me. And Hannie's father had taken their car to the repair shop.

"I guess we could have our tea party on the phone," I said.

"It will be a little hard to pass the cookies," said Hannie. "Anyway, I have to hang up now. Mommy is waiting for a call."

"Okay, see you at school," I said.

Boo. I wanted to have a tea party. I decided I would just have to have one by myself. I took my tea set and a tablecloth outside. I ran inside and got juice and cookies. I spread everything out on the front lawn. I was ready for my first guest.

"Dingdong!" I said.

"Coming!" I replied.

I opened my make-believe front door for my make-believe guest.

"Hello," I said. "I am so glad you could come for tea. Hannie is sorry she could not make it. Of course, that means we will have extra cookies."

I guess that was not very polite. But my guest did not seem to notice. At least she did not say anything.

I showed my make-believe guest to her seat.

"So, what is new?" I asked in my make-believe-guest voice. I ran to the other side of the tablecloth to answer myself.

"School was fun today," I said. "We read a book called *Alice's Tea Party*. It was excellent. Are you ready for some tea and cookies?"

I ran back to my make-believe-guest seat to answer.

"Thank you, I would love some," I replied to myself.

I ran back to the other side to pour the tea and pass the cookies. I was getting tired of running back and forth. I stopped for a minute to eat a cookie.

That is when I noticed a girl on the lawn next door. She was standing all by herself, giggling. I wondered what was so funny. Then I realized it was me. I must have looked pretty silly running back and forth. I started laughing too.

Then I thought of something. Having a real, live guest would be a lot more fun than talking to myself.

"Hi!" I called. "Would you like to come to my tea party? I have plenty of cookies."

"Thank you!" the girl called back. And she headed my way.

The Name Game

"I never saw anyone have a tea party like that before!" said the girl.

"I usually have tea parties with my friend Hannie. But Mommy could not drive me to her house," I replied.

"Where does she live?" asked the girl.

I told her about my old street. Then I told her about moving and how Mommy and Daddy got divorced. I told her about school and Andrew.

She told me about the school she went to and about her mommy and daddy. She said she did not have any brothers or sisters or pets.

"I want to get a cat someday," she said. Then she added, "Hey, I do not even know your name."

"And I do not know yours," I said. "This is fun! We can guess each other's names."

"Okay," said the girl. "You look like Susan."

"Wrong!" I said. "My turn. You look like Elizabeth."

"Nope," said the girl. "I bet your name is Carol."

When I heard "Ca" I thought she was going to guess my name.

"Close, but wrong again!" I said. "Give me a hint, and then I will give you one."

The girl stopped to think. Then she said, "The second part of my name is something you do with your eyes."

"Blink!" I shouted. "Your name is Roblink!"

"No way!" said the girl, giggling. "Now you have to give me a hint."

"My name starts like the name you guessed last time," I said.

"Um, Susan? Is your name Suellen?" said the girl.

"No. Susan was your first guess. Okay, now it is my turn," I said. "You *see* with your eyes. Your name is Tracy!"

"No, it is not," said the girl. "I remembered the name I guessed. It was Carol. Your name is Katherine!"

Just then, my mother opened the door and stepped out. Before I could stop her, she called, "Karen, are you ready for some lunch?"

"I got your name! It is Karen and I am a genius!" said the girl.

"Very funny," I replied. "Now you have to tell me your name."

"I do not. I want you to guess it."

"You did not guess my name. If you want to be my friend, you have to tell me yours," I said.

The girl was quiet for a minute. Then she said, "My name is Nancy."

"That is a nice name," I said.

"I like yours, too."

Then I called, "Mommy, can Nancy come for lunch?"

"Of course," replied Mommy.

Nancy ran home to make sure that was okay. It was. She ate lunch at my house. I ate dinner at hers.

I felt like the luckiest kid in the world. Now I had two great friends, and one of them lived right next door.

13

Goosie and Moosie

After awhile I got used to living at the little house and visiting the big house. But it was not so easy at the beginning. I did not like leaving Mommy. And sometimes I would forget things at one house or the other. (I was not a true two-two yet.) The first time Andrew and I went back to the big house, I forgot my toothbrush.

"We have plenty of extras," said Daddy.

I chose a pink-and-blue-striped one. It was pretty, but it was grown-up size and too big for my mouth.

Another time I forgot my pajamas. Hannie was sleeping over anyway, so she brought me a pair of hers.

But there were two things I *always* needed to have with me. I needed Tickly, my special blanket, and Goosie, my stuffed cat. I could not sleep without them.

One night Daddy was tucking me in at the big house.

"Wait, I have to find Tickly," I said.

I looked on my bed. No Tickly. I looked on the floor. No Tickly. I looked all around my room. No Tickly!

"We will find it in the morning," said Daddy.

"I have to have Tickly now," I said.

We looked everywhere but could not find Tickly.

"We have to go back to the little house," I said.

"All right, Karen. Put your coat on over your pajamas and we will go," said Daddy.

By the time we were downstairs, I was crying and cranky. So was Andrew. Daddy was unhappy because it was way past my bedtime. But we were going to go back to the little house anyway. We just had to. I opened the car door. The light came on.

"Tickly!" I shouted. My blanket was on the floor of the car. "I knew I did not forget you!"

"Well, that is a good thing," said Daddy.

We hurried back upstairs. I undressed and went to sleep with Tickly on my right side and Goosie on my left.

The next morning, I tore Tickly in half. I took half to the little house and left half at the big house. That way I would never be in either place without my special blanket. Unfortunately, the next week I forgot Goosie.

"Oh, Karen, not again," said Daddy.

"At least it is not bedtime," I replied. (I realized Goosie was missing as soon as we got to Daddy's house.)

"Maybe Goosie is in the car. Remember when you thought you lost Tickly?" said Daddy. We looked in the car. But Goosie was not there.

"I will drive you over to Mommy's," said Daddy.

At Mommy's house, Daddy rang the bell. Mommy was not home. Daddy found his keys so we went inside. Goosie was not at the little house either!

"I lost Goosie!" I cried. "I will never see him again!" I began to cry.

"We will go back and look at the other house," said Daddy. "I am sure he is there."

I was still crying when we pulled into the big-house driveway. Mommy was just getting out of her car. She was holding Goosie.

"You left him in the living room when you ran back for your sweater," said Mommy.

"Thank you!" I said. I was very happy to have Goosie back. But I started crying all over again.

"What is wrong?" asked Mommy.

"I am afraid I will leave him behind again. And I cannot tear him in half like Tickly."

Mommy and Daddy had a grown-ups'

talk. When they finished, Daddy said, "Come, we will go downtown and see if we can find another stuffed cat like Goosie."

We drove to the toy store. There, behind all the other stuffed toys, was a cat that was Goosie's twin. Mommy and Daddy bought him for me.

"Thank you!" I said. On the way back to the big house, I named my new cat.

"Goosie, meet Moosie," I said when I was in my room.

My life as a two-two had begun.

Meeting Seth

"We have so many books in this house," said Mommy. "I think we need to have some bookcases built into our walls."

"I want to help," I said. "I build good castles."

"You are a very good builder, but I think we are too busy to do this ourselves," said Mommy. "I am going to call a carpenter."

Mommy looked in the phone book under C for *carpenters* and found an ad she liked.

"What does it say?" I asked.

Mommy read me the ad. (I was only four

and a half, so I could not read it myself yet.) It said:

Need something built or repaired?
For Fast, Friendly, Fair Service
Call Seth Engle
Licensed Carpenter

Mommy set up an appointment for ten o'clock Saturday morning. When the doorbell rang and Mommy opened the door, I was surprised. I do not know why, but I was expecting someone old. But the man at the door was only old like Mommy. They smiled at each other.

Then they talked about where the bookcases should go. Once they had decided, the carpenter said he could start as soon as he had the proper materials. He came back the next Saturday.

"Do you need me to help you?" I asked.

"I am sure you are a very good helper," he said. "But you have to ask your mommy. These tools can be dangerous."

66

"It is all right," said Mommy. "I will watch you."

The carpenter told us to call him Seth.

"You can call me Karen. My mommy's name is Lisa!" I said.

It was my job to pass Seth his tools. I had to be careful. The hammer was heavy and the nails were sharp. (It was good that Andrew was napping. He was too little to help with important building jobs.)

While Seth and I were working, Mommy and Seth were talking. They were laughing a lot too.

Seth worked until lunchtime. Then he said, "I have another job now. I will have to come back and finish this on Monday."

When he came back on Monday, we were just starting to fix dinner.

"Are you sure you can do the job without me?" I asked.

"It will be hard, but I will do my best," said Seth.

I liked Seth. I could tell Mommy did too. After he left, she looked sad. We were about to eat our dessert when the doorbell rang. It was Seth again.

"I am sorry to bother you. I forgot my hammer," he said.

"It is no bother," said Mommy. "Would you like to join us for dessert?"

"Thank you, I would love to," he replied.

We were having apple cake that Mommy, Andrew, and I had baked together.

"This is delicious!" said Seth.

On his way out, Mommy asked Seth if he could build bookcases in my room too. I did not even know I needed them.

"Sure. I see your stair railing needs mending too. I will do that for nothing," said Seth.

Seth came around a lot after that. Mommy kept thinking of things that needed building. And Seth found lots of things that needed fixing.

Hmm. Something was going on.

Flower Girl: Part One

One Sunday Seth came over without his toolbox. Instead he brought presents for Mommy, Andrew, and me. Andrew and I got silly animals made out of wood. We loved them. Mommy got three wooden flowers painted in bright colors.

"Thank you. These flowers are beautiful," she said.

Seth spent the day with us. We walked around downtown and stopped for ice cream. Later we bought food at the supermarket and cooked dinner together.

Seth spent a lot of time with us after that. We really liked him and I knew he liked us. He even said he wanted to marry us! At first I was a little scared.

"What about Daddy?" I asked Mommy one night after Seth went home.

"You will always have your daddy, who loves you. Nothing will change that," replied Mommy.

She explained that if she and Seth married, Seth would be my stepfather. "Seth is another person who loves you and wants to take care of you," said Mommy.

That did not sound too bad to me. The next time Seth came over, I said, "Yes, we will marry you!"

Mommy and Seth laughed and hugged. Then came the fun part — the wedding! I got to be the flower girl. This was a very important job.

On the Sunday before the wedding we all had to go to the church and practice walking down the aisle. It was like getting ready for a school play. Only I did not get to say anything. At least I was not supposed to. But being quiet is hard for me.

"Should I walk fast or slow?" I called from the back of the church. Mommy came back and walked down the aisle with me.

"You need to walk slowly with the music," she said.

"Okay, now I will do it myself!" I said.

I ran to the back again. When the music started, I did not walk. I decided to skip. It is hard to skip slowly. I reached the front of the church in no time.

"Karen, we do not skip in church," said Mommy. "Please try walking again."

"But a wedding is happy," I said. "So is skipping."

"We need you to walk slowly so everyone can see how beautiful you look with the flowers," said Seth.

Seth always knows what is important. That is one of the reasons I like him. I ran to the back and called, "I am ready!"

The music started. I took one step and waited. Then I took another step and waited some more. I was only halfway down the aisle when the music ended.

"That was great," said Seth. "We can always play more music."

I practiced at home. I practiced at the Little Friends Day School. Finally, it was the day of the wedding.

"Do not be nervous," said Mommy.

"I am not nervous one bit!" I replied.

The church was filled with people. I could hardly wait for the music to begin. When it did, Mommy nodded and I started to walk down the aisle. I was wearing a gigundoly beautiful dress. It was long and pink with ruffles. I was carrying a big bouquet of flowers.

I did not walk too fast. I did not skip. I did not walk too slowly. I walked with the music, just like Mommy said. Everyone was smiling at me and I was smiling back.

It was the most fun day. After Mommy and Seth were married, it was time for the party. We held it outside in the park. (We

had tents in case it rained. But it did not. The weather was beautiful.)

We ate and danced and I got too many kisses. But I did not mind. After all, you have to expect lots of kisses when you are the best flower girl in Stoneybrook.

Kristy Thomas

One weekend, when Seth was away and Andrew and I were at Daddy's, Daddy got a phone call. He said hello, then got a worried look on his face.

I got scared. Daddy does not look worried very often.

"Daddy?" I said. I wanted to know what was wrong. Daddy motioned for me to wait. I started bouncing up and down. I could not stand still.

Then I heard Daddy say, "I will get someone to stay with Karen and Andrew. I will be over as soon as I can."

Daddy hung up and turned to Andrew and me.

"Everything will be all right," he said. "There is no need to worry, but Mommy hurt her ankle and she is at the hospital. I need to go there and help her."

Andrew started to cry.

Daddy took Andrew and me in his arms. "Mommy will be all right," he said. "Sometimes we fall. We may get hurt, but then we get better."

Daddy picked up the phone again and made a call.

"Hello, Elizabeth," he said. "Could Kristy baby-sit for Karen and Andrew? I can pick her up and bring her here."

(I had not met Elizabeth or Kristy yet.)

"Thank you," said Daddy. He hung up the phone. "Come on, kids. Someone very nice is going to stay with you."

We drove to a house on the other side of town and a girl got into our car.

"Hi, Karen. Hi, Andrew. I am Kristy. Your daddy has told me a lot of nice things about you."

"Hi!" I replied. I did not get to say much else. Daddy was doing all the talking. He was telling Kristy what we should have for lunch and where emergency phone numbers were.

"I wish I could take time to show you everything," he said. "Karen will have to fill in for me. Okay, pumpkin?"

"Okay!" I replied.

Daddy dropped us back at our house, then drove off to the hospital. Kristy, Andrew, and I went inside.

"Do not worry. I am a very good helper! I will show you everything in my house," I said.

"Maybe we should eat some lunch first," said Kristy.

That sounded like a good idea. I had eaten only a little breakfast. Toast and orange juice. I was hungry. Andrew said he was hungry too.

I went to the kitchen and started taking food out of the refrigerator. Cold cuts. Cheese. Tuna salad. Cole slaw. Apples. Carrots. Milk.

"Whoa! Your daddy said peanut butter and jelly sandwiches," said Kristy.

"That is for Andrew. I like everything!" I replied.

Kristy made sandwiches and cut up apples and carrots. She put the food on our plates so it looked very pretty.

"Yum!" I said. "You are a good babysitter."

"I have not done too much yet, but thank you," said Kristy. She poured the milk and we sat down to eat.

I took a few bites of my sandwich, then suddenly felt like crying. I looked at Kristy.

"Will our mommy be all right?" I asked.

"Of *course*," replied Kristy. "She hurt her ankle, but that is not too terrible a thing to happen. Even if she broke it, she will be okay. I once broke my ankle too."

"How did you do that?" I asked.

"While you are eating I will tell you," said Kristy.

I picked up my sandwich and took another bite. I was starting to feel better already.

"Here is my story," said Kristy. "I was riding my bike and my dog, Louie, was on his leash —"

"You have a dog?" I said. "Can I see him sometime?"

"Sure," said Kristy. "Anyway, I was taking Louie for a walk when —"

"Ooh! Can I walk him?" I asked.

"I guess," replied Kristy. "Are you going to let me finish the story?"

I nodded.

"All right, then. I was on my bike and Louie was beside me when I came to a tree. Louie went one way and I went the other. *Whoosh!* I flew off my bike and broke my ankle," said Kristy.

I started giggling.

"That was silly!" I said.

"It was not silly when I had to wear a cast

for six weeks and could not go swimming all summer," said Kristy. "But you are right. It sounds pretty silly now."

I liked Kristy. She was nice. I thought she was nice even before she gave Andrew and me ice cream for dessert.

After lunch, we played outside. Then, while Andrew was napping, Kristy read stories to me. We were reading *The Little Engine That Could* when Daddy walked through the door.

"Mommy is going to be fine. She is home and will call you soon," said Daddy. "How did everyone here get along?"

"Fine," I said. "I like Kristy! Does she have to go home?"

"Not yet. We have to wait for Andrew to wake up before I drive Kristy home," said Daddy. "Kristy, is that all right with you?"

"I do not mind at all," said Kristy. "Karen and I are having a very good time."

Kristy looked at me and smiled. I felt a lot better than before. Mommy was going to be fine. And I had the best baby-sitter ever.

The Witch's Spell

Kristy baby-sat for us lots of times after the day Mommy hurt her ankle. She got to know our house pretty well.

At first I only told Kristy nice things about our house. I wanted to be sure she came back. But on her third visit I decided to tell her about the witch next door. It was for her own safety.

"Um, I hope this will not scare you away," I said. "But there is a witch living next door."

"Really?" asked Kristy. She looked as though she did not believe me.

"Yes. Daddy thinks her name is Mrs. Porter. But her real name is Morbidda Destiny," I said.

"That *does* sound like a witch's name," said Kristy.

"She dresses in black and casts spells. Once she cast a spell on Boo-Boo. That is why he is wild," I went on.

"Well, then, I will watch out for Boo-Boo and for your neighbor. Thank you for warning me," said Kristy.

A couple of weeks later, Morbidda Destiny struck! Kristy was baby-sitting for Andrew and me. We were having a snack in the kitchen. Andrew was putting globs of jelly on crackers. And Kristy was looking for a jar of peanut butter when she bumped her head on a cabinet door.

"Ouch!" she said.

"Kristy get boo-boo!" cried Andrew.

Boo-Boo came into the room then. He must have thought Andrew was calling him. He rubbed against Andrew's chair.

Grape jelly from Andrew's crackers dripped onto Boo-Boo's tail. *Mee-owww!*

Boo-Boo licked his tail furiously. Then he started chasing his tail and would not stop. He jumped up on the counter, then down to the floor. Things were falling over. Boo-Boo was making a gigundo mess.

"Catch him!" I said.

"I will try my best," said Kristy.

She grabbed two oven mitts and put them on.

"No! I said catch him, not cook him!"

Kristy started to laugh. "I am putting the mitts on so I do not get scratched."

"Oh," I replied. Kristy was pretty smart.

But she was not smart enough to catch Boo-Boo. He ran out of the kitchen and into the living room. *Crash!*

Kristy, Andrew, and I peered around a corner to see what had broken. Oops. It was a blue vase.

"Boo-Boo running!" said Andrew.

"He is under a witch's spell!" I exclaimed.

"I think it is an angry cat spell," said Kristy. "Cats do not like having sticky jelly on their tails."

Boo-Boo was flicking his tail and spraying grape jelly all around the house.

"We will have to wait till he calms down," said Kristy.

Crash! Bam! Bang! Just then the telephone rang. Kristy answered it.

"Yes, Mrs. Porter. Everything is all right. Thank you," she said and hung up.

"Aha!" I cried. "It was Morbidda Destiny, checking on her spell!"

"I do not think so. Mrs. Porter called to see if we could use help. She heard all the noise," said Kristy.

"That is what she *said*. But I know better," I replied.

After Kristy hung up the phone, Boo-Boo stopped running around. I knew it was because Morbidda Destiny had called off her spell.

Boo-Boo sat down and licked the little bit of jelly that was left on his tail. Kristy cleaned up the house. I helped her. When we finished, Kristy said, "Except for the broken vase, everything looks fine."

"Until the next spell," I said. "I hope you were not too scared. Will you come back?"

"Of course I will come back," said Kristy. "I am not scared of crabby cats or witch's spells. And when things go wrong, I know I have a very good helper. Thank you, Karen."

Kristy looked at me and smiled. Even a witch's spell could not change that.

Flower Girl: Part Two

Not long after the witch's spell, Andrew and I met Elizabeth, David Michael, Sam, and Charlie.

We spent a lot of time together on weekends when Andrew and I stayed at Daddy's. So by the time Daddy told us he and Elizabeth were going to get married, we already felt like family.

By then, Andrew and I were also already two-twos. That is why I was not surprised that I was going to be a flower girl for a second time. (I am lucky. Some girls never get to be a flower girl even once.)

On the day of the wedding, I jumped out of bed.

"I am going to be a flower girl! Today is the day! Hooray!" I sang to Moosie.

I ate breakfast with Daddy and Andrew. Daddy gave us each a big hug.

"I will be pretty busy later," he said. "But you know where to find me if you need me. I love you both."

As we were finishing breakfast, Elizabeth, Kristy, and Nannie came over. (I had met Nannie a few times by then.) The four of us went to the spare bedroom. That way Daddy would not see Elizabeth getting ready. (Some people think it is bad luck for the groom to see the bride dressed before the wedding.)

Nannie helped me put on my dress. She had made it herself. It was short and yellow with lace on it. I had yellow shoes, white tights, and yellow and white flowers in my hair. I checked myself out in the mirror. I looked gigundoly pretty.

The wedding was going to be held in our backyard. The yard is big, so there was room for lots of people. As it turned out, there was one person too many. You will soon find out why.

When I was dressed, I went out to the yard. The guests were wearing their best clothes. There were flowers everywhere. (Daddy is a gardener and loves beautiful flowers.)

Kristy called, "Karen, come on! We are starting."

Suddenly I got butterflies in my stomach. Even though I had been a flower girl before, I was nervous.

Daddy stood in front of the minister. David Michael stood beside Daddy. (David Michael was the ring bearer.)

The rest of us were at the back of the yard. When the piano player began the wedding march, Sam said, "Here we go!" Sam walked Nannie down the aisle to her seat. Then he stood beside David Michael.

Kristy, the bridesmaid, was next. She walked down the aisle, then stood across from Daddy, David Michael, and Sam.

It was my turn. I started down the aisle. I tossed white rose petals first to one side, then to the other. I tried my best to walk in time to the music. Right foot, left foot. Toss, toss. Right foot, left foot. Toss, skip! Skip! Oops! I heard someone say I was adorable. I smiled and threw extra petals her way. I was having fun!

Elizabeth walked down the aisle behind me, holding Charlie's arm. Charlie brought her to stand beside Daddy.

The service began. I daydreamed through most of it. I woke up when I heard the minister say, "You may kiss the bride."

Daddy leaned over and kissed Elizabeth. Then people started getting up to congratulate them. That is when I screamed. Someone was heading in Daddy's direction holding a small box in her hand. It was Morbidda Destiny!

I started to shout, "Do not take it! It is a wedding spell!" Daddy covered my mouth with one hand. With his other hand, he reached out to take the box from his guest.

I was too scared to see what happened next. I pulled away from Daddy and ran to the house as fast as I could.

When I was brave enough to peek outside, Morbidda Destiny was gone and the wedding was going as planned. I found out later that a key ring was in the box. And no one seemed to be under any spells.

Morbidda Destiny is a witch for sure, but I think she is not a very good one. Except for Boo-Boo, none of her spells has worked yet. Thank goodness!

Ms. Colman's Class

Did you know that I am in second grade? Well, I am. Some kids my age are in first grade. I was in first grade for one week, then my teachers decided I belonged in second grade.

That is how I ended up in Ms. Colman's class. I love Ms. Colman. She is smart and nice. She never raises her voice, even though I give her lots of reasons to raise it. For example, sometimes I talk too loudly in class. Then Ms. Colman says, "Indoor voice, please, Karen." I try to remember that, but whenever I am excited I forget.

Ms. Colman is only one of the great things about my second-grade class. The other great thing is that Hannie and Nancy are in the class too. When I joined the class I got to sit next to them in the back of the room. Later, when I got my glasses, Ms. Colman moved me to the front so I could see better. But we are still together most of the time in school and out. That is why we call ourselves the Three Musketeers.

I remember the first day in Ms. Colman's class very well. It was an important day for me and for Hootie. Only Hootie did not know it yet. He was still in the pet store. And he was not even named Hootie. I will explain.

After I settled in that first day, Ms. Colman said, "Class, I have not forgotten about our problem."

I raised my hand. (Since it was my first day, I tried to behave myself.) "What problem?" I asked when Ms. Colman called on me.

Ms. Colman told me that the class had been trying to decide on a class pet.

"We cannot seem to choose between a hamster and a rabbit," said Ms. Colman. She said the class was going to vote again in case some kids had changed their minds.

I raised my hand again. A mean boy gave me a dirty look. But I did not care. I had already told him to leave me alone. And I told him, "You do not scare me." (The boy was Bobby Gianelli, by the way. He is not so much of a bully anymore.)

Anyway, I raised my hand and said, "What about a guinea pig? Guinea pigs are great pets. I played with one once. He was very, very friendly."

Guess what? The kids loved my idea!

"A guinea pig *would* be a good pet," said a girl. (It was Sara Ford, only I did not know her name yet.)

"I like guinea pigs," said a boy. (It was Hank Reubens.)

"Me too," said another girl. (It was Audrey Green.)

Ms. Colman wrote *guinea pig* on the chalkboard next to *rabbit* and *hamster*. Then she took a vote.

"How many of you want to get a guinea pig?" she asked.

There were sixteen kids in the class that day. Sixteen hands shot into the air. Yes!

A couple of days later we went to the pet store and picked out our guinea pig. We named him Hootie because he makes a loud whistling sound.

Hootie is happy in second grade. And so am I.

Karen's Book

I stopped writing my book and put down my pencil. My hand was stiff from writing so much. I shook it around.

It was late Sunday afternoon and the house was coming back to life. I had been writing for most of the weekend. I stopped for important things such as eating and sleeping. But the rest of the time I had stayed in my room and kept on writing. I did not mind because I was having so much fun.

"Hi, Karen," said Kristy, poking her head

around my door. "What did you do all weekend?"

I looked at all the pages on my bed.

"I wrote a book," I said.

"Really? That is amazing! Can I see it?" asked Kristy.

"Soon," I replied. "I am almost finished."

Kristy smiled and closed the door. I took out a special folder and put my book into it. I fastened the clasp and was about to write the title of my book on the front when there was a knock at the door.

"Hi, sweetheart," said Daddy. "Are you ready for dinner?"

"I will be down in a minute," I replied.

When Daddy left, I wrote the title of my book in big letters on the cover of my folder. Then I drew a picture and taped it below the title.

I went downstairs and slipped the book under my chair. I did not want anyone to see it until I was ready.

While we were passing around the

spaghetti, I said, "I have an announcement. After dinner I will be reading my book in the den. Whoever wants to hear it is invited."

"Are you going to read from a Paddington book?" asked Elizabeth.

"No, I am going to read my own book," I replied. "I wrote it all by myself."

"Then I want a front-row seat," said Daddy.

After dinner, everyone followed me into the den.

"Thank you for coming," I said. "I hope you like my story." (I heard an author say that at a bookstore once. I thought it sounded very nice.)

I held up my book and showed everyone the cover. It was a picture of me and my book. Then I began to read.

"*Little House, Big House: My Life Story*, by Karen Brewer," I said. Emily started clapping.

"Quiet, please. I have not even started the story yet," I said.

Nannie held Emily's hands in hers and I began to read.

" 'The Day I Was Born: Part One. It was a beautiful spring day,' " I said, and kept on going.

No one talked. No one fell asleep. Everyone listened. When I got to my last page, I read, " 'Hootie is happy in second grade. And so am I.' " Then I added, "The end. For now."

Daddy started clapping. Then Emily, of course. And Elizabeth, Nannie, Kristy, and David Michael.

"Bravo!" said Daddy. "I am so proud of you."

"That was a wonderful story," said Elizabeth.

"May I get a copy of your book?" asked Nannie. "I would like it signed by the author, please."

"So would I," said Daddy. "I will make copies for you. You can send one to Mommy, Seth, and Andrew in Chicago."

I could not believe it. I had written the

book just for fun. Now I felt like a real author.

"Everyone come to the kitchen for refreshments," said Elizabeth.

"I will come later. I want to write all this down," I said. I headed toward the stairs.

"Are you sure?" said Nannie. "We have cookies, ice cream, and homemade chocolates."

I turned back toward the kitchen.

"Yum! I want everything!" I said.

It was time for me to enjoy my first book party. Later, I could write all about it.

L. GODWIN

About the Author

ANN M. MARTIN lives in New York City and loves animals, especially cats. She has two cats of her own, Gussie and Woody.

Other books by Ann M. Martin that you might enjoy are *Stage Fright*; *Me and Katie (the Pest)*; and the books in *The Baby-sitters Club* series.

Ann likes ice cream and *I Love Lucy*. And she has her own little sister, whose name is Jane.

Little Sister

Don't miss #101

KAREN'S CHAIN LETTER

Hannie pointed. Oh my gosh! It was Ms. Agna! She was standing in our doorway talking to Ms. Colman. In her arms she held a big plastic sack.

"Karen?" said Ms. Colman. She motioned me to come over. She held the sack open for me to see. "Apparently you have received some mail at school," she said.

"My postcards!" I cried. "From my chain letter."

"Chain letter?" repeated Ms. Colman.

"Yes," I said. "It is sponsored by Kidsnetwork. These are postcards from all over the world!"

"Well," said Ms. Colman, "I can see that you are very excited. Perhaps you could share some of the postcards with the rest of the class."

LITTLE 🍎 APPLE

BABY-SITTERS™
Little Sister

by Ann M. Martin,
author of The Baby-sitters Club ®

More Titles... ➡

The Baby-sitters Little Sister titles continued...

☐	MQ48306-4	#61	Karen's Tattletale	$2.95
☐	MQ48307-2	#62	Karen's New Bike	$2.95
☐	MQ25996-2	#63	Karen's Movie	$2.95
☐	MQ25997-0	#64	Karen's Lemonade Stand	$2.95
☐	MQ25998-9	#65	Karen's Toys	$2.95
☐	MQ26279-3	#66	Karen's Monsters	$2.95
☐	MQ26024-3	#67	Karen's Turkey Day	$2.95
☐	MQ26025-1	#68	Karen's Angel	$2.95
☐	MQ26193-2	#69	Karen's Big Sister	$2.95
☐	MQ26280-7	#70	Karen's Grandad	$2.95
☐	MQ26194-0	#71	Karen's Island Adventure	$2.95
☐	MQ26195-9	#72	Karen's New Puppy	$2.95
☐	MQ26301-3	#73	Karen's Dinosaur	$2.95
☐	MQ26214-9	#74	Karen's Softball Mystery	$2.95
☐	MQ69183-X	#75	Karen's County Fair	$2.95
☐	MQ69184-8	#76	Karen's Magic Garden	$2.95
☐	MQ69185-6	#77	Karen's School Surprise	$2.99
☐	MQ69186-4	#78	Karen's Half Birthday	$2.99
☐	MQ69187-2	#79	Karen's Big Fight	$2.99
☐	MQ69188-0	#80	Karen's Christmas Tree	$2.99
☐	MQ69189-9	#81	Karen's Accident	$2.99
☐	MQ69190-2	#82	Karen's Secret Valentine	$3.50
☐	MQ69191-0	#83	Karen's Bunny	$3.50
☐	MQ69192-9	#84	Karen's Big Job	$3.50
☐	MQ69193-7	#85	Karen's Treasure	$3.50
☐	MQ69194-5	#86	Karen's Telephone Trouble	$3.50
☐	MQ06585-8	#87	Karen's Pony Camp	$3.50
☐	MQ06586-6	#88	Karen's Puppet Show	$3.50
☐	MQ06587-4	#89	Karen's Unicorn	$3.50
☐	MQ06588-2	#90	Karen's Haunted House	$3.50
☐	MQ06589-0	#91	Karen's Pilgrim	$3.50
☐	MQ06590-4	#92	Karen's Sleigh Ride	$3.50
☐	MQ06591-2	#93	Karen's Cooking Contest	$3.50
☐	MQ06592-0	#94	Karen's Snow Princess	$3.50
☐	MQ06593-9	#95	Karen's Promise	$3.50
☐	MQ06594-7	#96	Karen's Big Move	$3.50
☐	MQ06595-5	#97	Karen's Paper Route	$3.50
☐	MQ55407-7		BSLS Jump Rope Pack	$5.99
☐	MQ73914-X		BSLS Playground Games Pack	$5.99
☐	MQ89735-7		BSLS Photo Scrapbook Book and Camera Pack	$9.99
☐	MQ47677-7		BSLS School Scrapbook	$2.95
☐	MQ43647-3		Karen's Wish Super Special #1	$3.25
☐	MQ44834-X		Karen's Plane Trip Super Special #2	$3.25
☐	MQ44827-7		Karen's Mystery Super Special #3	$3.25
☐	MQ45644-X		Karen, Hannie, and Nancy The Three Musketeers Super Special #4	$2.95
☐	MQ45649-0		Karen's Baby Super Special #5	$3.50
☐	MQ46911-8		Karen's Campout Super Special #6	$3.25

Available wherever you buy books, or use this order form.

Scholastic Inc., P.O. Box 7502, 2931 E. McCarty Street, Jefferson City, MO 65102

Please send me the books I have checked above. I am enclosing $_____
(please add $2.00 to cover shipping and handling). Send check or money order – no cash or C.O.Ds please.

Name_____ Birthdate _____

Address_____

City _____ State/Zip _____

Please allow four to six weeks for delivery. Offer good in U.S.A. only. Sorry, mail orders are not available to residents of Canada. Prices subject to change.

BLS1097